LADYBIRD BOOKS, INC.
Auburn, Maine 04210 U.S.A.
© LADYBIRD BOOKS LTD 1989
Loughborough, Leicestershire, England

Printed in England

Rhyming Rabbit

By Joan Stimson
Illustrated by Carolyn Ewing

Ladybird Books

Why Ronnie Rabbitson rhymed was a mystery.

Ronnie's father was a man of few words. "Hold tight!" was his favorite phrase. "Next stop Haresville" was a long sentence for him. (Mr. Rabbitson was a bus driver.)

Ronnie's mother used plain language. "Chow time!" she cried at mealtimes. And, if she was a bit impatient, it was, "Not now, Ronald."

But right from the start, Ronnie was different.

Most rabbits' first words are "Mom" or "Dad"
or "MORE!" Ronnie's first words were:

> "Ain't it fun to be a bun?
> My rabbit days have just begun.
> There's lots to see and lots to do,
> And I will rhyme it all for you."

"Good heavens!" cried Mr. Rabbitson.

Mrs. Rabbitson blushed. She didn't want her
child hogging the conversation.

When Great-aunt Dora arrived for a visit, she
cuddled Ronnie and tickled him under the chin.
"Who's the handsomest little bunny in the whole
wide world?" she cooed.

Great-aunt Dora expected Ronnie to gurgle.
But Ronnie rhymed!

> "Oh, Auntie dear, you've made my day.
> What charming things you have to say!
> I'd love to stay here on your lap,
> But now it's time to take my nap."

"Good grief!" gasped Great-aunt Dora. "This rabbit's
not normal!"

But, except for his rhyming, Ronnie *was* normal. He played and got into scrapes and mischief just like any other little rabbit. And, just like any other little rabbit, sometimes he fell down and hurt himself. But he never cried or complained. Instead, he brushed himself off and declared:

"Oh, I don't mind a little fall,
And I won't cry, no, not at all.
As long as I can say a rhyme,
I'll end up happy every time!"

Ronnie's parents wondered where it would all end.

"Those rhymes will get him into trouble," said Mr. Rabbitson.

Mrs. Rabbitson agreed. "One day he'll say one rhyme too many," she said. "I'd better take him to the doctor."

"Now, what seems to be the trouble?" asked Dr. Pill.

Mrs. Rabbitson opened her mouth to explain. But Ronnie got in first.

"Oh, Doctor, Doctor, look at me,
I'm strong and healthy as can be!
I've got no spots, I've got no chills,
I climb up trees, I roll down hills.
Oh, Doctor, Doctor, can't you tell,
I'm nothing but completely well!"

"Goodness gracious!" cried Dr. Pill. "This rabbit needs an x-ray. I think he's swallowed a rhyming dictionary."

But Ronnie hadn't swallowed a rhyming dictionary.
The x-ray was clear.

"Ronnie will grow out of it," said Dr. Pill
at last. "Just give him this medicine."

Ronnie took all the Grow Out of It medicine.
But he still kept rhyming.

Finally Mr. and Mrs. Rabbitson decided to face
facts: Ronnie might never speak plain English.

One day, Ronnie's parents took him to the zoo. Ronnie loved it. And of course, he had a rhyme for every animal he saw.

"Don't get too close," said Mrs. Rabbitson when Ronnie was watching the lions.

Ronnie stood back from the fence and said:

"Oh, Lion, you're a super guy.
I'd like to look you in the eye!
But I mustn't get too near—
You'd soon be roaring in my ear!"

They got to the elephant enclosure just in time to watch Jumbo take his walk.

Ronnie looked up at Jumbo. Jumbo looked down at Ronnie. Then, suddenly, the elephant swooped the rabbit up in his trunk!

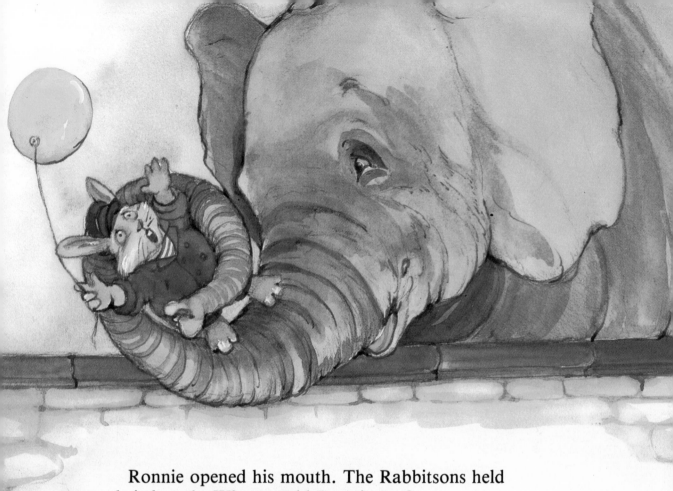

Ronnie opened his mouth. The Rabbitsons held their breath. What would Ronnie say?

Ronnie didn't hesitate. Out it all came in a rush: "HELP! STOP! LET GO! I'M A FLUFFY BUN, NOT A HAMBURGER BUN!"

Ronnie hadn't rhymed!

The keeper rushed out and rescued Ronnie.

Mrs. Rabbitson beamed with relief.

Mr. Rabbitson beamed with pride. "That's my boy!"
he said.

Ronnie was very quiet on the way home. He was subdued during supper. He asked to go to bed early.

Ronnie's parents went upstairs to tuck him in.

"Good night, Ronnie," whispered Mrs. Rabbitson.

"Good night, son," whispered Mr. Rabbitson.

They waited for Ronnie to whisper back....

But Ronnie didn't whisper at all. Instead, he sat up and said, at the top of his voice:

"Gosh!
That Jumbo-ride was pretty scary.
From now on I'll be much more wary!
This rhyming stuff might be okay,
But not if Jumbo comes your way.
If Jumbo gets you, yell and shout
Until you get the keeper out!
If you don't rhyme, it doesn't matter,
As long as someone brings a ladder!
Today I've learned that there's a time
And a proper place to rhyme!

"Good night, Mom and Dad."